N
W E
S

ARRAN
& BUTE

SKATE
BAY

BAY

HORSE
HILL

FARM &
CHAPEL

BALLOCHMARTIN
BAY

FINTRY
BAY

VIKING
LONGHOUSE

STANDING
STONE

V
I
K
I
N
G

G
R
A
V
E
S

CUMBRAE
TOWN

KAMES
BAY

MAIN
HARBOUR

THE POINT

LITTLE
CUMBRAE

GREAT
CUMBRAE

To Largs

WHITE BAY

SLATE BAY

ARRAN & BUTE

FARLAND POINT

Horse Hill

FINTRY BAY CHAPEL

GALLOCHMANTIOLL BAY

VIKING CROSSOVER

STANDING STONE

CUMBRAE TOWN

LAMB'S TAIL

FAIRHAVEN

The Eye

GREAT CUMBRAE

LITTLE CUMBRAE

Vikings and Skylarks on Cumbrae

Written by Maura McRobbie

Illustrated by Sophie Rowan

Printed in Great Britain by Bell and Bain Ltd, Glasgow

Dedication

This book is dedicated to all the children who have ever run wild and free on the Ayrshire hills, and particularly those on the island of Cumbrae. No matter what century, no matter who ruled, the feeling of roaming and breathing in the fresh sea air is timeless. And Viking warriors, who lie still beneath the earth, know you are there, and are whispering their tales too, if only you would stop awhile and listen.

 # Contents

 # Contents

Chapter One

Moranna's Island Home

he skylarks rose high in the sky, the buzzards circled their newly formed nests.

"Aaaah, yes," Moranna sighed. She so loved her beautiful island home. Riding bareback to the top of the island, on this clear fresh spring day, she could see the neighbouring islands unfold: Bute, Arran and Jura beyond. All set against each other, separated by slithering glints of sea. At the top of Cumbrae, Moranna reigned wild and free. She was majesty. But truly she belonged to Ballochmartin Farm. Her father was the farmer there, as were his father and grandparents before him. Ballochmartin was known to have the best farming land on Cumbrae, and had a quaint stone chapel, built where it was believed that Celtic saints in times gone by had worked and prayed. It was 1259, and Moranna was eleven years old.

On bright spring days like this, she'd often ride to the top of the island cantering amongst the yellow gorse and the springy heather. She enjoyed the wild, carefree feeling, before slowly taking her pony back down, being careful not to tread on any hidden rabbit holes. On the way home, she'd often spy on the Viking encampment. She'd done this since she was a little girl. Between the wooded pine trees, she would dismount, and holding on to her pony's reins, she would peer through the trees to see the smoke coming out of the longhouses, she'd hear the children laughing and playing, and the sound of chisels and hammers, as the craftsmen made their furniture and frames.

They were always busy doing something, she thought. They were always a bit mysterious too. Never mixing with the local people, only visible on occasions, like at the local markets in Largs, or when they were out fishing, and landing their catches into baskets on the jetties and piers. The locals recognised many of their faces, but rarely did they talk to one another.

Moranna's father always spoke highly of them. The Vikings, he said, had traded peacefully with the Scottish people for more than two hundred years now, and he always said they had brought prosperity to the island. Moving a bit closer, Moranna could see one of the boys working outside. It looked like he was stretching out sheepskins on the ground with large stones, before hanging them to dry on wooden frames. As he turned towards her, she recognised him as Sten. She had known him to be a younger Viking boy. She remembered seeing him fishing on calm summer days in the bay with a group of friends. She had also seen him sometimes down in the town on market day. She had heard his friends calling him Sten. He was growing up, she thought. He surely must be at least fourteen by now. As she watched him carefully stretching and smoothing out the sheepskins, she smiled to herself as she slipped away with her pony back to the safety of the farmhouse.

Chapter Two

The Sheepskin Waistcoat

It would soon be Moranna's twelfth birthday. Her mother had promised to buy her something new to wear at the next Viking market in Largs. It was exciting going on the large wooden sailing boat that was waiting at the eastern side of the island. The boat would cross over the narrow channel to Largs. It was packed with women and children carrying baskets and sacks ready to bring all that they were going to buy back home. Men too packed the boat talking about the latest implements they had seen

the Vikings use for mending and making things.

The bustle at the market was exciting too, with lots of stalls selling dishes, pots, pans, kitchen utensils, baskets, oil lamps, colourful woven cloths, and a multitude of implements and tools for fixing and mending things. Moranna's mother bought some new dishes for the farmhouse and some of the delicious Nordic butter that she swore was the best she'd ever tasted. She often wondered what their secret recipe was so that she could make it on the farm. Moranna had already made up her mind what she'd like for her birthday. She had often admired the sheepskin jackets and waistcoats that were for sale. She hoped that they would have one her size, and that it wouldn't be too expensive.

As they walked towards the stall, Moranna was secretly surprised to see that it was Sten along with another man serving. Their stall was laden with sheep and goatskin garments, pouches, belts and lots of rabbit skin hats and wraps. Sten's eyes lit up as he saw Moranna and for one embarrassing moment Moranna wondered if he knew that she sometimes secretly spied on him. He welcomed Moranna and her mother to his stall and Moranna noticed that he spoke good English, with a slight Nordic accent.

"Hello ladies, how can I help you?" he smiled.

"I'm looking for a waistcoat, sheepskin if possible for my daughter," said Moranna's mother hesitantly.

"I think I have just the perfect one," he said with a look of certainty, and he went into a box behind the long wooden tabletop where he produced a beautifully embroidered sheepskin waistcoat. "Try it on," he said, passing it to Moranna. She put it on over her woollen dress and she smiled delightedly,

"It fits! Oh mum, it's beautiful. Can I have it?"

"Oh, I'm sure you can my darling," said her mother lovingly, turning to Sten for the price.

"Two Nordic Crowns," he said, "that's the best I can do."

"Well, I'm sure I can manage that," said her mum, opening her leather pouch. "You see it's Moranna's birthday. She's twelve today and I promised her a treat. She's my only daughter, and she'll soon be grown up....." and she smiled lovingly at her daughter.

"It's your birthday?" said Sten brightly to Moranna. "Happy Birthday! I hope you have a very nice day. Now let me wrap your waistcoat, and as a special gift, I have a very special pair of sheepskin slippers – just your size – to match.   I would like to give you these as a birthday present."

"Oh no," said Moranna's mother. "You don't have to do that! No, no! You really don't."

"Not at all," replied Sten firmly. "She is your princess after all, and" he smiled looking for the words, "it is her birthday. It is my pleasure," and he wrapped the two items in a large linen bag that he tied securely before handing it over to Moranna to carry.

"Thank you so much," she beamed, her cheeks flushed and her eyes sparkling. "You have made my day!"

That night, back in the farmhouse, after telling her father all about the meeting with Sten the young Viking from the longhouse across the hill, Moranna went to bed. As she slept, she dreamt that she was a Viking princess, wearing a long cream dress with her beautifully embroidered waistcoat over it. Her chestnut brown hair was lightly covered in petals, and it was as if she was walking on clouds, or fluffy white sheepskins. What a dream, she thought! A Viking princess! And she smiled to herself as she sat down to breakfast with her mum and dad the following morning.

Chapter Three

Ships on the Horizon

our years passed, and Moranna was now sixteen. The sheepskin waistcoat was too small for her now, but she had worn it often. It was kept safely wrapped in its linen bag in a cupboard beside her mother's bed. She had kept the slippers too, although they were much too worn and should have been thrown out. But Moranna wanted to keep them. She still treasured them and that lovely day in Largs. She had seen Sten a few times, in the town, in Largs, sometimes out on horseback. She had often seen and heard her Nordic neighbours practising their

sword moves in the clearing outside the longhouse, and she wondered if Sten was one of them. She didn't have the courage to spy on them now, as she had done when she was younger.

"Do you think the Vikings would ever go to war again with us?" Moranna asked her father seriously one evening.

"No, no. Not now," her father replied. "They've settled in too well with us Scots. They live peacefully with us now, side by side. They even have passed good laws too that have been to our advantage, like making sure we have good land to farm and that we trade fairly with one another. No, I think they are here to stay for good. Why do you ask?"

"It's just that I hear them sharpening their weapons and practising their war moves outside the longhouse. I just wondered why."

"Oh, I'm sure that's just for fun. Or to keep up the pretence that they're still as fierce. They were violent warriors at one time, but that was a while ago now. I'd say their warring days are over. I don't think there will be any more battles," he said thoughtfully. Moranna hoped it was true.

That afternoon she took her pony up to the top of the island. It was a bright, windy afternoon and the skylarks were beating their wings and wheeling freely in the vibrant sunshine. Down below the sea sparkled a clear crystal blue with white roller wave crests. As she cantered freely along the hills and around the rocky crags, she felt glad to be alive. Looking down towards Largs she could see several Viking longships anchored in the bay. And in the distance, she could see what looked like a fleet of ships crossing the open channel between Arran and Bute. They didn't look like Viking ships though. Perhaps they were French or Scottish? They didn't have the colourful sails, or the sleek appearance of the Viking boats. They seemed to have different hulls and sails. An unusual sight, she thought and she wondered where they were heading. She must tell her father. He would know where they came from.

As she turned her pony round to make her way home, it momentarily lost its footing and stumbled. Moranna was thrown onto the ground where she lay dazed. As she tried to gather herself, she could hear voices in the distance. She recognised the language as Nordic. They were up to take a better look at the ships gathering in the distance. As they got closer, she was amazed to see that one of them was Sten. He saw that it was Moranna who had fallen. He knelt down beside her and spoke with concern, "Are you alright? Can you sit up? I saw what happened...... your pony has bolted. Don't worry, my friends will fetch it, and I will take you home. Be sure you can trust me. I will take you home." He carefully helped her to her feet, and together they walked slowly home while his friends went to catch her pony.

Over the next few months Sten visited Moranna's farmhouse frequently. He would call round to see how she was doing, and if her sprained ankle had healed. Moranna's mother and father welcomed him, and he began to join them for evening meals and chats around the fireside. When her ankle had mended, they'd go riding high to the top of the island on their ponies, stopping at rocky crags to watch the birds' nests and the sun go down over the sleepy peaks of Arran. They'd share stories of their lives and experiences. Sten told her about the Viking Gods Freya, Odin and Thor, while Moranna told him about Christianity and the three beings in one God: the Father, the Son and the Holy Spirit. Sten visited the little stone chapel next to the farmhouse, and Moranna visited his longhouse. Everyone made a great fuss of her. The menfolk were friendly and funny. The womenfolk showed her the strong colourful fabrics they'd woven and treated her to homemade cakes with a warm, sweet milky drink. Moranna even got to see where the children slept, in little beds down the side of the longhouse.

told him about Christianity and the three beings in one God: the Father, the Son and the Holy Spirit. Stort visited the little stone chapel next to the farmhouse, and Moranna visited his longhouse. Everyone made a great fuss of her. The menfolk were friendly and funny. The womenfolk showed her the strong, colourful fabric they'd woven and treated her to homemade cakes with a warm, sweet milky drink. Moranna even got to see where the children slept in little beds down the side of the longhouse.

Chapter Four

King Haakon and Sten

Moranna and Sten enjoyed being together. Sten began to tell her how he came to live on Cumbrae. One evening as they sat high up on the hills overlooking Fintry Bay towards Arran, he explained that his mother and father had died when he was young and that he had been raised by his aunt, who lived in the Viking settlement on Cumbrae. He told Moranna that his mother's brother, his uncle, was a very important Viking, and that he visited him on Cumbrae once or twice a year.

"Even though I don't see him often, I know he loves me very much, and it makes up for the loss of my mother and father," he said wistfully.

"How did they die?" asked Moranna.

"They were shipwrecked – on a journey to the north, where they were hoping to resettle and I would join them, but I was only a baby, so it was my aunt on Cumbrae who raised me."

"So who is your uncle then?" asked Moranna.

"He's actually King Haakon, and he comes to the island for the Viking parliaments - they sometimes meet over there on that island," and he pointed to the Little Cumbrae. "It's usually once or twice a year."

"A Viking parliament?" asked Moranna curiously. "What is that?"

"It's where the noblemen meet to agree laws, to work with the Scots, and to continue living in peace. You must notice the longships gathering across the water."

"Ah yes, I do know what you mean. So, your uncle is really King Haakon then?"

"Well yes, it's a bit embarrassing," hesitated Sten, "because I don't feel royal or noble at all."

"But your mother was his sister, does that mean she was a princess?" Moranna was confused.

"I'm sure she was, but after my mother died, I was happy to live here with my aunt and my cousins, my father's family, who were not

Royal in the least. There was no need for me to live elsewhere. My uncle, King Haakon always made sure that I learned to speak English and that I learned all the true skills of being a noble Viking."

"Like what?" asked Moranna, settling back on the grassy slope.

"Like fishing, hunting, sheep-shearing and stretching, leather-making, metalworking, woodcrafting, housebuilding, being good at almost everything......even the art of war."

"Like sword–fighting and being fierce in battle?"

"Yes, exactly. And that's what I've been learning for the past few years. No longer passing my days selling sheepskin waistcoats!

Do you still have that one I sold you at the market in Largs?"

"Yes, perfectly preserved in my mother's large cupboard," laughed Moranna. "I will keep it always to show my children and my grandchildren, and my grandchildren's children, and tell them that a Royal Viking Prince sold it to me when I was twelve years old!!!" Moranna's eyes twinkled at the thought. But more seriously she asked Sten about war and battles.

"What about that fleet of ships we saw on the horizon the day I fell off my pony? Does that mean there might be battles in the future? My father seems to think we can all live in peace."

"It's not as simple as that," said Sten sadly. "I wish it was. We Vikings have heard that the Scots, under King Alexander, want rid of us. They want to send us back to Norway, we are no longer wanted in Scotland. That's why all those ships have gathered recently. They're King Alexander's fleet and they've sailed round from the east coast."

"Will you need to go back to Norway then?" asked Moranna anxiously.

"Not without a battle. As you know we Vikings live in peace now. We are no longer the dangerous warriors we once were, but we would need to defend our longhouses and land in Scotland. We don't want to be forced out, but the Scots are making life more and more difficult for us."

"Oh, surely not!"

"Longships are being prepared now Moranna. It is something we will all have to face. I have heard that my uncle is on his way too, and that means we must be prepared for battle soon."

Chapter Five

The Battle Begins

nd just as Sten had said, King
Haakon arrived on the island
of Cumbrae, and let his
fellow Vikings know that a battle date had
been set for 2nd October 1263. On the
morning of the battle, King Haakon, Sten
and many other noble Vikings attended
Mass at the little stone chapel at
Ballochmartin Farm. King Haakon prayed
for a peaceful solution and that not too
many lives would be lost before taking up
position in his longship off the coast.

Sten was amongst the 800 warriors
who landed on the shores off Largs and went

into battle with the Scots soldiers who swarmed in their thousands over the Ayrshire hills, down towards them. As the fierce battle cries went up and the clash of swords flashed on the beaches, it became clear that the Viking warriors were significantly outnumbered. King Haakon could see his men fall one by one, and still more Scots warriors were pouring down over the hills. By admitting defeat early, he decided, more lives would be saved. If he and his men tried to retreat, the Scottish fleet of ships were out in the channel ready to attack. No, the only solution was to admit defeat and give Scotland the freedom they wished for. He signalled for his men, those that remained alive, to lay down their weapons and admit defeat.

Sten was on the rocky shore when he saw the signal from his uncle's longship. He too had realised the huge number of Scots soldiers, and that he would soon be facing death. There seemed to be thousands of them, fearsome, angry, all ready for the kill. Their battle cries were blood-curdling, and he knew he was no match for them as his ancestors must have been. He thought of his loving, thoughtful uncle, his peaceful life on Cumbrae and Moranna who he knew would be watching from her hilltop viewpoint on her pony. He stumbled on the shoreline, and throwing down his sword and shield before him, he lay behind a large red sandstone rock and pretended to be dead. Motionlessly, he prayed that he would not be discovered. Silently, from the corner of his eye, he saw his sword and shield being snatched by a Scots soldier as a trophy of the battle. Quietly to himself he whispered, "Take it! Take it! But please leave me my life."

45

Chapter Six

Viking Graves

he following morning Sten gradually awakened to the cry of gulls swirling overhead and waves gently lapping to the shore. As he slowly opened his eyes, he began to make sense that the battle was over and that he was still alive. As he looked around, he saw that he was surrounded by many dead Viking warriors. Some still had their weapons by their sides. Others had their helmets on. Sten recognised some of them as friends he had lived and worked with in the longhouse. He sat on the shore with his head in his hands. He was

devastated by the loss. In the distance he saw his uncle's longship coming towards him. He could see the distinct golden dragon figurehead and the gold, red and white sail that signified his royal status. Shattered by the experience, he stood up slowly and walked to the shoreline where the water lapped at his feet. King Haakon came ashore and hugged him tightly and gave thanks to God for the safety of his nephew. The two men then walked sadly through their fellow warriors who lay dead, shaken by the aftermath of the battle.

"We will give them a full warriors' burial," said King Haakon solemnly. "I want them to lie here forever in peace. Life was so peaceful for them here in these parts. I want them to be buried beside the wildflowers, near the heather and the gorse bushes, and somewhere where they can always see the sea. For that is what Viking warriors were truly made for.....to be Earls of the Sea!"

"I know exactly the best places for them," said Sten, "over there, high up on the hills of Cumbrae," and he pointed across to his island home. "That's where they should be buried and almost everywhere you go, you find a view of the sea. Let's bury them there."

And that is what they did. King Haakon, Sten and the surviving Vikings lifted each warrior one by one, placed them into the longship, and sailed them over on their final journey where they laid them to rest surrounded by the glittering sea, sand and sky on the hills of Cumbrae overlooking Fintry Bay. Some were laid to rest with their weapons intact. Others were buried simply in their warrior clothes, just as they'd fallen. At each burial, they said a Nordic prayer, and a Christian prayer, to make sure they had the blessing of all the Gods. Then King Haakon urged Sten and the survivors to make haste, to gather the women and children in the nearby longhouses, to get on board his longship and to hasten their retreat to Norway.

"There's no time to delay," said King Haakon. "King Alexander's men will be at our tails unless we make haste!"

"Oh, I wish I could stay," said Sten, thinking of his life on the island. "I have been so happy here. It is the only home I have ever known."

Chapter Seven

King Haakon's Farewell

arly that evening they gathered the women and children who had already begun to pack. Many of them were grief-stricken. They knew that their menfolk had died. They had seen the victory fires of the Scots burning late into the night across the water and they had heard the ferocity of the Scots victorious chants. They knew it was bad news for the Vikings. But Sten and his men kept their spirits up, urging them to make haste and board the longship in the bay. There was no time to be lost. As the procession of women

and children with all their packed goods made their way through the town, the local people came out to watch their final departure.

"I never thought this day would come," said Moranna's father sternly after leaving the town. Moranna was in the farmhouse sobbing. She was certain Sten had been killed in the battle and she was very upset.

"Why did all this have to happen? They were so peaceful and happy here. I hate the Scots soldiers," she wept.

"It had to happen I suppose," said her father quietly. "But don't distress yourself, lass. Many of the Vikings survived and I'm sure Sten is among them. They're all gathered at the harbour at the moment, preparing to leave."

"Sten" she cried in disbelief, "you mean he's at the harbour and he's alive!"

"Well, I can't be sure, but I think I saw him. There was a great commotion at the pier when the longship with the Royal Flag came in.... all the womenfolk are making their way down now. The longship is about to set sail for Orkney I believe."

"I've got to see Sten before he leaves," shouted Moranna as she ran out of the door and flew down the hill towards the bay.

It was a chaotic scene when Moranna arrived. Everyone was making their way onto the Royal longship, carrying all their belongings in bundles and baskets. She scanned every face looking for Sten. Surely, he would come and see her if he was still alive? Surely, he wouldn't leave without saying goodbye?

Meanwhile Sten was talking seriously to his uncle on the harbour beside the gangway.

"Do I have to leave? Would it not be possible for me to stay and to keep a small Viking settlement on the island?"

"Of course not Sten! There is no future here now for Vikings. You will almost certainly be killed," he warned. A look of despair came over Sten's face and he looked towards the ship, but just as he turned his head, he heard a voice calling,

"Sten! Sten! You're alive. I don't believe it! I was so sure you were dead," and Moranna ran straight into his arms, hugging him and sobbing with relief.

"I very nearly died," he whispered into her hair as he held her, "but I am safe. Oh Moranna, I wish I could stay here with you. But I must leave Cumbrae forever. It is not safe for me anymore."

"Oh, don't go Sten, please stay. You can come and live with my mother and father on our farmhouse. Father could do with a hand, especially as I'm his only daughter... oh please Sten, please say that you'll stay. You know you can live in peace with us."

Sten turned to his uncle with a pleading look.

"Uncle, what do you think? Could it be possible?"

"It's your decision," said King Haakon seriously. "If you choose to stay on Cumbrae and live as man and wife with Moranna and her family, you should be able to live in peace with the Scots people for the rest of your life. You have already settled well with them. Your ways and their ways are similar. But remember, your children and your children's children will be Scots. They will never be Vikings or know of their Viking roots."

"Of course, they will know, because I will tell them often," said Sten, visualising a future on Cumbrae, surrounded by love and a family in the farmhouse with Moranna.

"Well then Sten, you must make your decision. We will set sail at dawn. Your future will be determined by then. Whatever you decide, I will always love you."

Sten looked at Moranna. She was smiling, gently tugging him, willing him to stay.....she hadn't even asked her mother and father, but she knew they would welcome him with open arms.

"Alright," said Sten bravely, "my decision is made. I'm going to stay. I'm going to stay and make my future on Cumbrae."

The following morning, as the longship sailed off, Sten waved farewell to King Haakon, with Moranna smiling happily by his side. King Haakon waved a final farewell to his nephew, to the island of

Cumbrae and to Scotland. Not long after, in Orkney, he would pass away, content in the knowledge that his young nephew had found happiness with his love on Cumbrae.

Sten and Moranna were soon married in the little stone church next to Ballochmartin Farm and this was followed by a celebration party on the beach with all the locals from the island. Over the next few years, they stayed at the farm helping with all the daily tasks. But later, they decided to move across the hill into the longhouse that had been lying empty since the Viking departure and that Sten had begun to repair. They had four children and now and again when Sten and Moranna would go walking with them over the hills, they'd lay flowers at the graves of the Viking warriors who had lost their lives at the Battle of Largs.

And to this day, Sten and Moranna's descendants still run wild and free on the island of Cumbrae, while the Viking warriors lie deeply asleep, beneath the gorse and heather surrounded by the glittering sand, sea, and skylarks of Cumbrae.

The End

The End

Historical Background

"From the ninth to the thirteenth centuries Bute, Arran and the Cumbraes were strategically located islands in a maritime world of mixed ethnic identity. They were frontier islands where Norse and Scottish culture met and where national political ambitions clashed." Barbara Crawford, Honorary Reader, University of St Andrews, Honorary Professor of the Highlands and Islands University, Nordic Studies from 'The Norse in the west with particular reference to Bute'

The ingredients for my story 'Vikings and Skylarks on Cumbrae' is a mixture of historical evidence, word-of-mouth folklore, and sprinkled with a little bit of imagination. As a writer, I make no apologies for being inspired by the historical facts to create a story that might or might not be true. However, for those seeking the facts, I have put together some of the evidence as best I can. For those who have the history of the Cumbraes at their fingertips, I apologise if I have made any errors and I am happy to be corrected.

1. The name Cumbrae comes from the Gaelic, meaning a shelter or a refuge. It is sometimes referred to as Cambray; Cimbray, or Cimbrae: the place of the Cymric people. An alternative theory states that the name originates from the word Kimmora, (Keil-Maura) which means a church dedicated to St Maura.

2. The islands of Bute, Arran, the Cumbraes, Islay, Jura, Gigha, Colonsay, part of Kintyre and the Isle of Man once formed part of the Norse Kingdom, known as Sodor and Man.

3. This kingdom was distinctive in that it held frequent parliaments to decide laws and regulations relating to the sea and land. Currently it is thought that the Parliament may have been in Bute. However, it could also have been on the island of Little Cumbrae, which had a castle, and was where Scottish nobles in the 1300s, after the Battle of Largs, signed laws. The Little

Cumbrae was also known as a Christian place of pilgrimage and worship, where St Beya had lived and preached around 600s AD. There is a shrine to St Beya on the island.

4. The Cumbraes are situated off the west coast of Scotland and hold a strategic position at the estuary of the River Clyde where it narrows and allows access to the upper Clyde and deep water lochs beyond. The Cumbraes lie closer to the mainland than their neighbouring islands of Bute and Arran and are much smaller.

5. The isles are made up of Great Cumbrae, Little (Wee) Cumbrae and the Eilans. Great Cumbrae is around 4km in length and 2km wide. The town of Millport lies to the south of Great Cumbrae, and because of the relatively small size of the island, the entire island is often called Millport.

6. Little Cumbrae lies off the southern tip of Great Cumbrae and is a rough and rocky island with the remains of a castle and a lighthouse.

7. The Eilans are two smaller islets situated in Millport bay and are currently home to colonies of seals.

8. A Norse settlement was believed to have been situated at Foulport to the west of the island, opposite Little Cumbrae. It was named thus as the place of 'tall men' – 'foulesport'. This is around the location of the current boatyard in Millport.

9. In 'Vikings and Skylarks on Cumbrae', I decided to locate the Viking encampment on the east side of the island, in the sheltered woodland area off Ferry Road, not far from Ballochmartin Farm. This seemed a perfect, secretive location for all the wood-skills and crafting the Vikings excelled in, and it is also nearer the Standing Stone, where ancient peoples would have lived with exceptional viewpoints over the Clyde estuary. However, as sea-farers, it is possibly more likely that the Vikings settled nearer 'Foulport'.

10. The Islands of Cumbrae are mentioned in the mediaeval Norse Saga of Haakon Haakonarson and

referred to as '*Kumreyiar*'.

They hosted a mixture of settlements and cultures: Gaelic/Scots/Christian/Norse and were historically located in the Gall- Gaedhil territory.

11. King Haakon met with Scottish nobles before the Battle of Largs in 1263 to try and come to an agreement about the ownership of the Gall-Gaedhil territory. The talks failed and resulted in the Battle of Largs in 1263.

12. A Mass took place in a chapel in the grounds of Ballochmartin Farm which was attended by King Haakon and his nobles before the Battle. After the Battle, King Haakon retreated to Orkney, and died shortly after, as is recorded in the Viking Sagas.

13. Before retreating, many Viking warriors were buried on the island of Cumbrae and some were burned on the Norwegian ships before they sank.

14. Great Cumbrae, with its rich pastoral and fertile lands, suitable for grazing and growing crops has been known to have been inhabited since the last Ice Age.

15. Some say the isles of Cumbrae have an Ecclesiastical history as rich as and as equal to that of Iona with several Early Christian shrines where people worshipped and prayed.

16. At Upper Kirkton, the site of the original Christian settlement, shrines and stonework have been found and are now displayed at the Cathedral of the Isles.

17. Another shrine was found where the former church stands at the top of Churchill Street. A further shrine was located on the present site of the Cathedral of the Isles.

18. A monk's cell/cave, believed to be that of St Martin's, was located at Balloch Bay near the grounds of Ballochmartin.

19. There have been Christian settlements on the isles of Cumbrae since 500 AD. St Columba is believed to have visited the island sometime around 600s AD.

20. Saint Maura, was a Scottish saint who is said to have died in 899 AD. She lived and worked on the isle of Cumbrae and was thought to be the daughter of a Scottish Chieftain. It was recorded that St Mirin ridded the islands of snakes and set up a monastery with St Baya and St Maura.

21. The early Christian churches of Cumbrae passed to the Diocese of Paisley in 1160, almost a century before the Battle of Largs. The Norse rulers and the Christian communities had found a way to live in peace and harmony for the benefit of all.

The isles of Cumbrae may be small and less significant in size to their island neighbours, but they are rich in Gaelic/Scots/Norse culture. In writing the story, 'Vikings and Skylarks on Cumbrae,' I wanted to use this rich history and culture to inform readers of the important stories that are within our grasp. With a little leap of the imagination, I created the characters Moranna and Sten, who became friends, and whose lives were affected by the outcome of the Battle of Largs. I wanted to create a story that depicted this harmonious and peaceful life. It is not beyond the realms of possibility that a Scots lady or girl had a Viking warrior as a husband or friend. Indeed, on a final note, there is evidence of a Lady's Grave on Great Cumbrae, where legend has it, there lies the remains of a Lady, who died broken-hearted on hearing of the death of her Viking Warrior husband, at the Battle of Largs.

Maura McRobbie
2022

References
With grateful appreciation to 'The Isles of Cumbrae, Old and New, A Short History' by Archibald Templeton McConnochie, 1964, a small leaflet that cost 15p back in the day, and is a treasure of information.
'Welcome to Wee Cumbrae' Limited Edition by John and Noreen Steele, 2009
The Geology and Folklore of the Island of Cumbrae, Map and Tour Guide

 # Acknowledgements

I would like to thank Pamela Hanlon for her
invaluable comments and her lifelong knowledge and
love of the island of Cumbrae. I would like to thank
the children I taught, who told me they would love to
read a story about what it would be like for Scots
children to live alongside the Vikings in Scotland.
This was my motivation to write the story.

Maura McRobbie is a writer of Scottish/Irish descent. Her first novel Howth was published in 2019 and is the semi-biographical story of her grandmother Florrie who grew up in Dublin in the early twentieth century.

Maura lives in Bearsden outside Glasgow and her holiday home is on the island of Great Cumbrae off the west coast of Scotland. This is where the inspiration came for her first children's novel: Vikings and Skylarks on Cumbrae. The story was Highly Commended by the Scottish Association of writers and there are Teachers Notes and associated merchandise available on her website: www.mauramcrobbie.com

Sophie Rowan is an illustrator living in Glasgow, originally from North Lanarkshire. Having graduated from The Glasgow School of Art in 2019, she has worked on a variety of projects from table top games to children's books.

You can find more of her work on her website:
cargocollective.com/sophierowan